# CAMP WONDERFUL WILD

by LAUREL SNYDER illustrated by CARLYNN WHITT

Amazon Children's Publishing

AMAZON PUBLISHING
ATTN: AMAZON CHILDREN'S PUBLISHING
P.O. BOX 400818
LAS VEGAS, NV 89140
www.amazon.com/amazonchildrenspublishing

Library of Congress Cataloging-in-Publication Data available upon request.

ISBN-13: 9781477816523 (hardcover)
ISBN-10: 1477816526 (hardcover)
ISBN-13: 9781477866528 (eBook)
ISBN-10: 1477866523 (eBook)

The illustrations are rendered digitally.
Book design by Vera Soki
Editor: Robin Benjamin

Printed in China (R)
First edition
10 9 8 7 6 5 4 3 2 1

SHOFAR BOOKS

For Jacqueline Carper Podowski, who took me to camp
—L.S.

For kids of all ages who step away from their screens
and into the wild
—C.W.

There are monsters in the wild.

There are loads of chores to do.

There are buzzing, stinging, winging things. . . .

There's muck and mud and goo.

There are topple-down disasters

that ruin *everything.*

In the morning, much too early . . .
there are songs you *have* to sing.

There are little kids who follow

and big kids who won't play.

Plus rainy nights and soggy shoes
and ghosts to scare away.

There are goofy hats and dances
and days without dessert.

TONIGHT!

FIDDLER
ON THE ROOF:
7:30 P.M.

✳

S'MORES:
9:00 P.M.

HONEY
GRAHAM

CHOC

HONEY
GRAHAM

MARSH-O

MARSH-O

There's no TV for miles around.

NATURE
SCAVENGER
HUNT!
• PINECONE
• SHELL
• BEETLE
• SPIDERWEB
• SOMETHING
  BLUE
• SOMETHING
  WITH SPOTS

GOOD LUCK!

You need to stay alert!

There are rafts you'll *never* get to.

There are trees you'll never climb.

Then grueling hikes up mountains . . .

and getting left behind.

But the most horrible thing of all,
the worst thing that I know . . .
The very hardest part of camp . . .

is when it's time to go.